Belinda's New Spring Hat

FRANKLIN WATTS, INC.
575 Lexington Avenue
New York, N. Y. 10022

Eleanor Clymer

BELINDA'S NEW SPRING HAT

Pictures by Gioia Fiammenghi

For Jane Emily

Library of Congress Catalog Card Number: 69-11524
© Copyright 1969 by Eleanor Clymer
Printed in the United States of America
1 2 3 4 5

It was spring. The birds were singing. The flowers were blooming.

6

All the ladies had new spring hats. They were going to wear them on Sunday.

Mother—

Aunt Jane—

Cousin Ruth—

Grandma.

Belinda watched them all as they tried on their hats.

She said, "I would like a new spring hat, too."

Mother said, "Of course you would. We will get you one."

"When?" Belinda asked.

"Well, not today," said Mother. "But soon. Just wait."

Belinda waited.

All the time she was playing, and eating lunch, and resting, she waited.

At last she decided not to wait any longer.
"I'll have to find a hat myself," she thought.

9

So she began to look for one. She looked in her
room first, and right away she found something.
"Here's a good hat," she said, and she put it on
her head and went to show Mother.

"Why, Belinda!" said Mother. "What's that on your head?"

"It's my new spring hat," said Belinda. "How does it look?"

"It looks lovely," said Mother. "It looks like a lampshade."

Belinda looked in the mirror. It did look like a lampshade. She put it back on the lamp and went to find something else.

This time, she looked in the living room.
"Here's a good hat," she said. And she went to show Aunt Jane.

"Why, Belinda!" said Aunt Jane. "What's that on your head?"

"It's my new spring hat," said Belinda. "Is it all right?"

"It's fine," said Aunt Jane. "But it's rather large, almost like a wastepaper basket."

Belinda tried to look in the mirror again, but she couldn't see.

She lifted her hat and peeked. It did seem to be a wastepaper basket. She put it on the floor. And she picked up the pieces of paper that had fallen out of it. Then she looked around some more.

She looked in the kitchen.

"This ought to make a good hat," she said. And she went to show Grandma.

"Why, Belinda!" said Grandma. "What is that on your head?"

"It's my new spring hat," said Belinda. "Do you like it?"

"It's charming," said Grandma. "Only it does look a little like the cat's basket."

Belinda sighed. It *was* the cat's basket. She put it back, and the cat got into it.

"I *must* have a new hat," said Belinda, "or I'll have nothing to wear on Sunday. I'll look again."

She looked in the hall closet.

"Maybe this will do," she said. And she went to show Cousin Ruth.

Cousin Ruth was just getting ready to go out. She was hunting for something.

When she saw Belinda she said, "Why, Belinda! What is that on your head?"

"It's my new spring hat," said Belinda. "Does it look nice?"

"It looks like my shopping basket," said Cousin Ruth. "May I borrow it to go shopping?"

"Okay," said Belinda. She took it off and gave it to Cousin Ruth.

"But what shall I do for a hat?" she wondered.

She looked on the porch. "Oh! How about this?"

Just then, someone came up the steps. She ran to see who it was.

It was Daddy, and he had two packages, one under each arm.

"Hello, Daddy," said Belinda.

"Why, it's Belinda," said Daddy. "What is that on your head?"

"It's my new spring hat," said Belinda. "How do you like it?"

"Very becoming," said Daddy. "And it's different. There won't be another girl with a hat like that."

Belinda smiled from under the hat. You could trust Daddy to say the right thing.

Then she looked at the packages.

"What have you got there, Daddy?" she asked.

"Oh," said Daddy, "this is a rosebush for Mother. Would you like to help me plant it?"

"Of course," said Belinda. "In what?"

"In a flowerpot, of course," said Daddy. "I bought one specially."

"Where is it?" Belinda asked.

"In this box," said Daddy. And he gave Belinda the other package.

Belinda pulled off the string. She took off the lid. She looked inside. There was tissue paper.

"What a funny way to wrap a flowerpot!" she said.

She pulled out some tissue paper,

and more tissue paper,

and more tissue paper.

And there, in the bottom of the box was—

"A flowerpot," said Daddy.

"Daddy! You're not going to plant a rosebush in that!" said Belinda.

"You think not?" said Daddy. "Perhaps you're right. What shall we do? It's too late to buy another."

"Take my hat," said Belinda.

"Sure you don't mind?" said Daddy.

"Not a bit," said Belinda.

"Well, all right," said Daddy, "if you insist. But you'll have to wear the flowerpot."

"I'd love to," said Belinda.

And on Sunday, she did.